For Ashley x

Visit the author's website: www.ericjames.co.uk

Written by Eric James
Illustrated by Sara Sanchez and Darran Holmes
Designed by Nicola Moore

Copyright © Hometown World Ltd. 2018

Published by Sourcebooks Jabberwocky, an imprint of Sourcebooks, Inc.
P.O. Box 4410, Naperville, Illinois 60567-4410
(630) 961-3900
Fax: (630) 961-2168
jabberwockykids.com

Date of Production: October 2017
Run Number: HTW_PO250717
Printed and bound in China (IMG)
10 9 8 7 6 5 4 3 2 1

Tiny the Boston Easter Bunny

Written by
Eric James

Illustrated by
Sara Sanchez

sourcebooks
jabberwocky

One bright Easter morning,
while out for a jog,

Tiny hears,

"HELP!
I AM STUCK
IN A LOG."

He scratches his head,
thinking, "Who could that be?
It sounded like Fluff!
I had better go see."

Fluff's in a log
with her feet in the air.
"Hey, Fluff, what on earth
are you doing in there?"

A sad little voice
from an echoey space
says, "I thought this would make
a good egg-hiding place."

"You poor Easter Bunny,"
says Tiny, while giggling.
"I'll get you back out,
just hold tight and stop wriggling!"

Tiny pulls hard,
using all of his might.
He tries and he tries,
but his friend is stuck tight.

"My eggs," sighs poor Fluff.
"Who'll deliver them now?"
"I'll do it," says Tiny.
Fluff laughs and asks,

"How?!"

"Don't worry, dear Fluff.
Leave it all up to me.
I watched you last Easter.
How hard can it be?"

This bunny looks funny... Yes, something is wrong!

His feet are **too big** and his nose is too **long.**

His skin isn't **furry,** it's wrinkled and rough.

His tail is **too thin,** and it's **NOT** made of fluff.

He's traveled through **Fenway**
and **North End** already.
He's all out of puff
and his legs feel unsteady.

He **hops**, then he stops,
then he **hops** a bit more,
then he stops all the **hopping...**

The Boston Bookshop

SWEET TREATS

MASSA-CHEW-SIT CAFÉ

and **FLOPS**
to the floor!

"Hello," squeaks a mouse
in his fake bunny ear.
"Oh my, how you've grown
since I met you last year.
I'm Marvin, remember?
You're running quite late...
I'll help if you like."
Tiny nods and says,

"Great!"

They head down to **Somerville**,
rush through the streets,
delivering handfuls of
chocolatey treats.

Next **Charlestown**, then **Chinatown**,
Beacon Hill too.
There's not much time left
but there's SO MUCH to do!

"Speed up," Marvin squeaks,
"or we'll finish too late!
DIG under that hedge and
HOP over that gate."

This **Lexington** house
has a fence all around.
Poor Tiny tries digging
down into the ground.

But the hole is too small (or his body's too big).
"How odd," Marvin thinks. "I thought bunnies could **dig!**"

This large **Back Bay** house has a really high wall. "Jump up," Marvin squeaks. "C'mon, give it your all!"

So Tiny jumps up but comes down with a **THUMP!** "How odd," Marvin thinks. "I thought bunnies could **JUMP!**"

"There's something not right,"
Marvin says. "Let me see..."
He scratches his chin and thinks,
"What can it be?"

"You're not very fast—
well, just look at those legs!
You're not very careful.
You've cracked half the eggs!"

"You do not have whiskers!
You're no good at hopping!
Those ears look quite fake,
and that's **no** bunny dropping!"

"Aha! Now I've got it!"
He jumps to his toes.
"No bunny is born with a
trunk for a nose!"

Tiny starts crying.
He wails, "Yes, it's true!
I thought I could do the
things real bunnies do."

"Don't worry. It's fine!"
Marvin squeaks, being nice.
"Do you mind if I offer
a little advice?"

"You need to start using
the talents you've got.
Be proud to be **you**.
Don't be something you're not!"

Public Garden

"What talents?" says Tiny.
"What things can I do?"
He blows his big nose
and then aah...

aaah...

ACHOOOOOO!

"Eureka!" squeaks Marvin
from high in a tree.
"That wonderful,
big trunky nose
is the key!"

"It's strong and it's long.
It can pick things up, too.
It's perfect for seeing
this Easter job through."

"We'll put it to work
just as soon as we can.
Let's head down to Dorchester,
test out this plan."

This house has a fence,

and this house has a wall,

but with Tiny's big nose, there's no problem at all!

His long nose lifts up,
reaches over the top,
and he drops an egg down
on the lawn with a

P
l
o
P!

And look at the hole
in this fence...that'll do!
There's room for an egg
and a trunk to fit through.

Now the job seems quite easy. (Well, that's how it goes
when an elephant uses his brains and his nose.)

But daylight is breaking.
The sun starts to rise,
and home after home
stands in front of their eyes.

"I don't think we'll make it,"
squeaks Marvin. "Oh, dear!"
"Hang on," Tiny shouts.
"I've a marvelous idea!"

He sucks all the Easter eggs
into his nose,
and when his trunk's full
he takes aim...then he BLOWS!

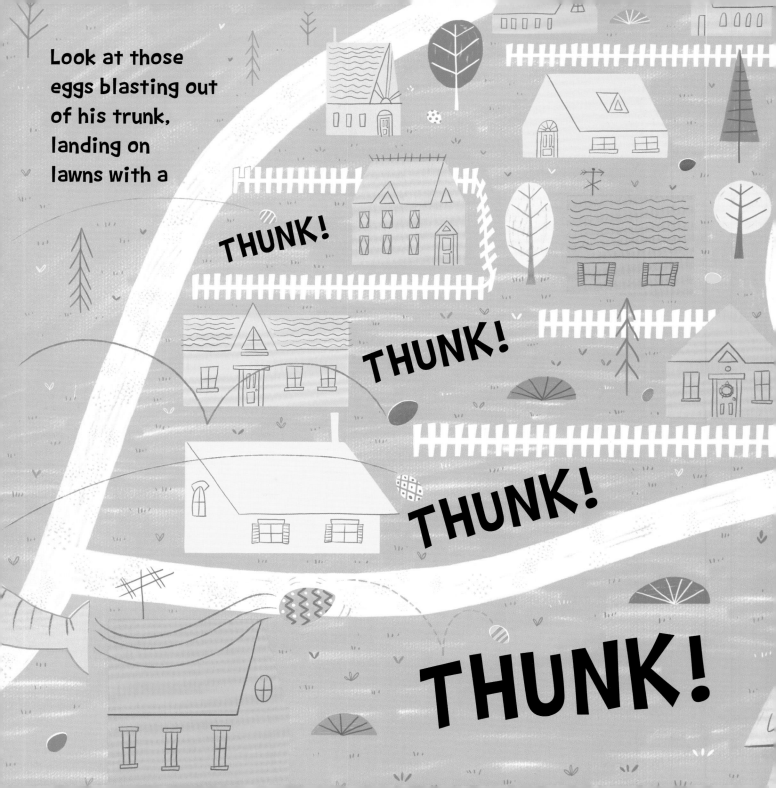

Look at those eggs blasting out of his trunk, landing on lawns with a

THUNK!

THUNK!

THUNK!

THUNK!

The basket's soon empty.
"We did it, hooray!
Come on, let's help Fluff.
Oh, I hope she's okay."

At the side
of the pond,
Tiny dips in
his trunk.
He drinks and
he drinks
till the water's
all drunk!

And using
his nose
as a huge
water hose,
he blows
through the log...

Look at Fluff!

UP
she goes!

Happy Easter, Boston!

How many Easter eggs
are in this picture?